Louise Fatio

The World in the Candy Egg

by ALVIN TRESSELT

The World in the Candy Egg

illustrated by

ROGER DUVOISIN

Lothrop, Lee & Shepard Co., Inc. New York

High on a shelf in a toyshop sat a candy egg.

Spun of sugar,

covered with rosebuds,

touched with magic,

with a big glass window in the end of it.

Inside, the bottom was green grass,

and a pale spun-sugar sky was the top.

A tree grew beside a little house

where an old woman baked bread in the kitchen,

and little kittens played on the doorstep.

Two storks built their nest of twigs and straw

on the chimney top.

A shepherdess watched her sheep by the side of a brook,

and a shepherd chased crows in the cornfield.

Secret world, magic world, spun of sugar and light,

Where the old woman bakes and the kittens play,

The sheep nibble grass and the crows fly away, fly away, fly away,

In the magical world of the egg.

A tiny bird peeked into the egg.

She saw the long-legged storks
guarding their nest on top of the chimney.

And she watched the kittens

tumbling on the doorstep.

A chicken looked into the egg.

She saw a cricket hide behind a leaf.

She saw a beetle resting on a rock.

And she watched a caterpillar crawl up a blade of grass.

A woolly lamb looked . . .

He heard the cool brook bubbling in the meadow.

He saw the shepherdess nod her head

as she sat under the tree daydreaming.

He saw birds sitting on the fence.

He saw cabbages growing in the garden.

And he saw butterflies dance over a clump of chicory.

Little world, tiny world, where everything's snug and tight.

A butterfly sips at a milkweed flower

While the shepherdess rests in her meadowy bower,

The sheep nibble grass and the crows fly away, fly away, fly away,

 In the magical world of the egg.

A doll with bright blue eyes looked into the egg.

She saw the little shepherd trip on his stick

as he chased the crows from the cornfield.

She saw the old woman sweeping the kitchen floor.

Then one day the shopkeeper took the egg down from the shelf.

She put it in a box filled with soft white tissue paper.

She wrapped it up and tied it with a big yellow ribbon

on the outside.

Now it was dark in the egg.

No pale spun-sugar light filled the little world,

and nothing happened for a long time.

The old woman stopped baking.

The crows didn't caw

and the bubbly brook didn't run.

The shepherd and shepherdess stood beneath the tree.

The sheep didn't graze, and even the butterflies' wings were still.

Quiet world, hidden world, dark as the darkest night.

The bread doesn't bake and the brook doesn't run,

The shepherd and shepherdess wait for the sun.

The sheep are asleep, and the crows fly away, fly away, fly away,

In the nighttime world of the egg.

Then suddenly the wrappings rustled and crackled!

Snip—the ribbon was cut. Off came the cover,

and the soft tissue paper was folded back.

A little girl picked up the egg

and carefully she lifted it out of the box.

Gently she held it as she peeked inside.

And there was everyone busy working again !

The old woman was baking her bread.

The sheep were nibbling grass while the shepherdess watched.

The shepherd chased the cawing crows,

and the butterflies danced over the chicory.

The little girl saw the storks strut back and forth on the rooftop.

She smiled as the shepherdess stroked a baby lamb.

She laughed to see the kittens turn somersaults on the doorstep.

And the little world of the egg belonged to the little girl.

Magic world, little world, made for a child's delight,

Where time doesn't pass and it never gets cold,

And the shepherd and shepherdess never grow old . . .

The sheep nibble grass and the crows fly away, fly away, fly away,

In the make-believe world of the egg.

This book is set in CASLON *types by* FROST BROTHERS, *New York; lithographed in full color by* REEHL LITHO, *New York; and bound by* SENDOR BINDERY, *New York.*

Louise Fatio